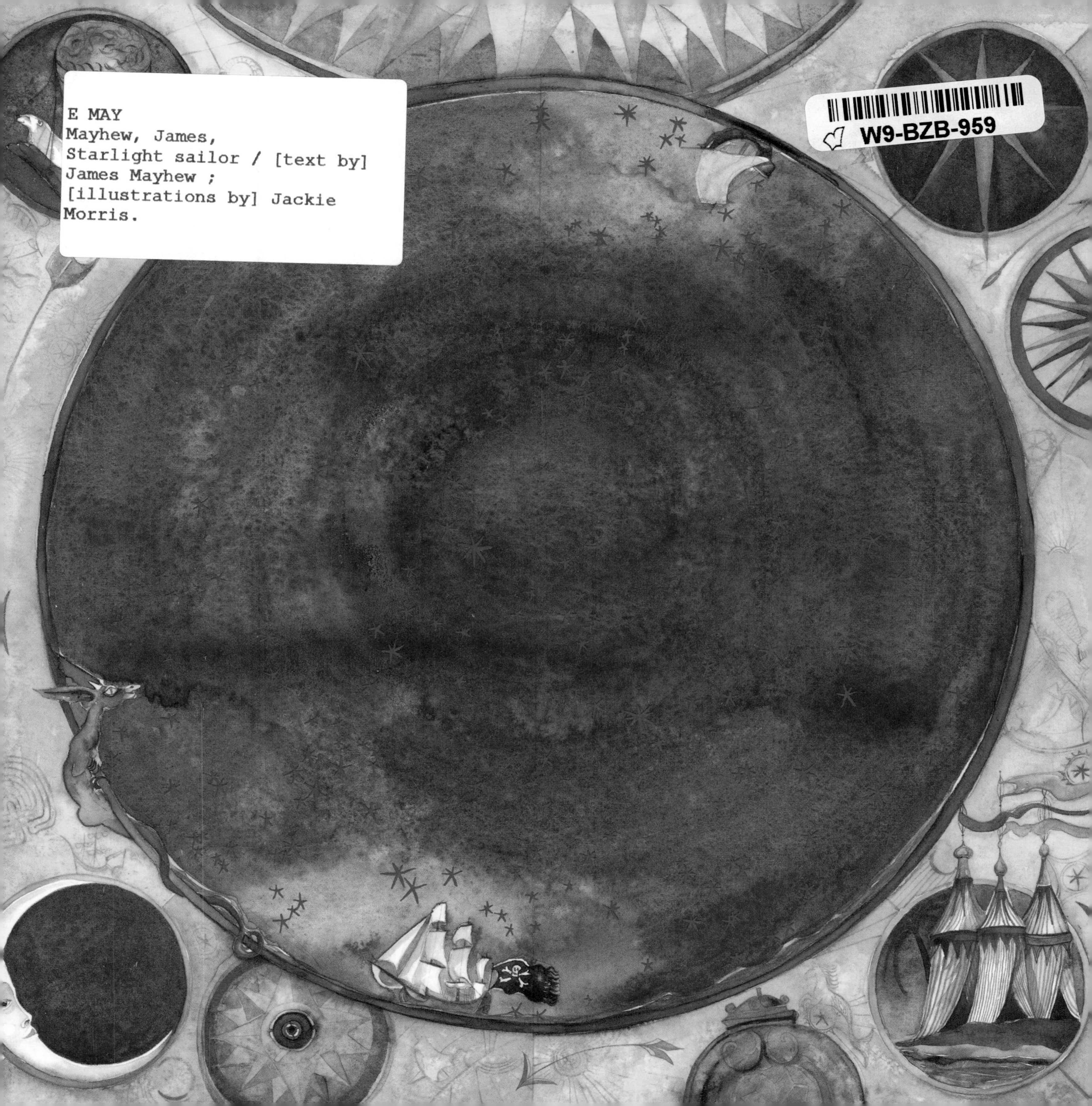

For Gabriel with his starlight wishes — James Mayhew

For Madgeanna Scully, born on the 24th July 2006, may your dreams be always filled with starlight and your wishes come true.

And for Jurianne Matter, maker of wish boats — Jackie Morris

Barefoot Books Ltd
124 Walcot Street
Bath, BA1 5BG

Barefoot Books
2067 Massachusetts Avenue
Cambridge, MA 02140

Text copyright © 2009 by James Mayhew
Illustrations copyright © 2009 by Jackie Morris
The moral right of James Mayhew to be identified as the author and Jackie Morris
to be identified as the illustrator of this work has been asserted

First published in Great Britain in 2009 by Barefoot Books, Ltd and
in the United States of America by Barefoot Books, Inc

This book has been printed on 100% acid-free paper
Printed and bound in China

This book was typeset in Albermarle, Bernhard Modern, Harrington and DellaRobbia

Hardback ISBN 978-1-84686-185-7

British Cataloguing-in-Publication Data: a catalogue record for this book is available from the British Library

1 3 5 7 9 8 6 4 2

Library of Congress Cataloging-in-Publication Data
is available under LCCN 2008028137

STARLIGHT SAILOR

Barefoot Books
Celebrating Art and Story

Star light, star bright,
First star I see tonight,
I wish I may, I wish I might,
Have the wish I wish tonight.

I wish I had a little boat!

Far away I drift and float,

Where the great blue whales leap,

And pirate ships lie sunken deep.

I sail towards another land,
Where children wait on golden sand.

"Over here!" the children say,
"We hope you want to come and play!"

We build a castle
high as high,

With flags that flutter
in the sky,

And let the sea fill up the moat,
Then play upon my little boat.

Up above a bluebird sings,
While we pretend we're knights and kings.

Being very strong and brave,
We go exploring in a cave.

We meet a dragon, red and gold,
Who tells us magic tales of old,

Then stretches both
her wings out wide,
And takes us on
a night-time ride.

We fly across the starlit sky
Until it's time to say goodbye.

Then she brings us down to land
Gently on the golden sand.

Now the children fall asleep.
The dragon curls up at their feet.

I climb aboard my boat once more,
And drift out slowly
                    from
                          the
                               shore.

Starfish swimming in the sea,

Mermaids singing just for me,

I listen to their lullaby,
While flying fish dance in the sky.

Star light, star bright,

First star I see tonight,

I follow you across the night,

through my dreams...

... 'til morning light.

Make your own Paper Boat

Fold a piece of paper in half towards you.

Fold down the top corners so that they meet in the middle.

Fold up the bottom edge of the top sheet of paper.

Next, fold the corners over.

Turn the paper over and do the same on the other side.

Open out the triangle shape to make a hat.

Then fold the hat down flat to form a kite.

Fold the upper bottom point of the kite up towards the top.

Then turn the paper over and repeat.

You now have a triangle shape again.

Open the paper out to make a hat again. Then fold it down the other way to form a kite again.

Carefully open out the paper boat by holding the two top points and pulling them gently to the sides.

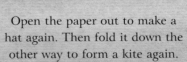

Your boat is now ready for its first voyage!

Barefoot Books
Celebrating Art and Story

At Barefoot Books, we celebrate art and story that opens
the hearts and minds of children from all walks of life, inspiring
them to read deeper, search further, and explore their own creative gifts.
Taking our inspiration from many different cultures, we focus on themes that
encourage independence of spirit, enthusiasm for learning, and sharing of
the world's diversity. Interactive, playful and beautiful, our products
combine the best of the present with the best of the past to
educate our children as the caretakers of tomorrow.

Live Barefoot!
Join us at www.barefootbooks.com

Jackie Morris lives in a little house by the sea where she paints, draws and dreams and makes paper boats. She shares her life with her two children, Tom and Hannah, three dogs and too many cats. Jackie has illustrated and compiled *The Barefoot Book of Classic Poems* (2006) for Barefoot. She has also illustrated many other books, written a few, and won the odd award or two.

At night Jackie watches the patterns in the stars and wishes on the ones that fall. If she could have a wish come true it would be that she had a time machine so that there could be more hours in the day for drawing and painting, writing and dreaming.

James Mayhew is a professional daydreamer, turning his imaginings into stories and pictures for children. He works in a garden studio where he can watch his son playing in his tree house and listen to grand opera.

He has previously illustrated *Shakespeare's Storybook* (2001) and *The Barefoot Book of Stories from the Opera* (1999) for Barefoot, and is passionate about introducing children to art and culture.

When he isn't working, James bakes cakes for his wife.

Share your own paper boat adventures at www.barefootbooks.com